Anansi and the Moss-Covered Rock

retold by Eric A. Kimmel

illustrated by Janet Stevens

Holiday House /New York

To Jonny

Text copyright © 1988 by Eric A. Kimmel
Illustrations copyright © 1988 by Janet Stevens
All rights reserved
Printed and Bound in October 2012 at Tien Wah Press, Johor Bahru, Malaysia
24 26 25
Library of Congress Cataloging-in-Publication Data

Kimmel, Eric A.
Anansi and the moss-covered rock / retold by Eric A. Kimmel:
illustrated by Janet Stevens. — 1st ed.
p.   cm.
Summary: Anansi the Spider uses a strange moss-covered rock in the
forest to trick all the other animals, until little Bush Deer
decides he needs to learn a lesson.
1. Anansi (Legendary character)   [1. Anansi (Legendary character)
2. Folklore.]   I. Stevens, Janet, ill.   II. Title
PZ8.1.K567An 1988
398.2′452544—dc 19
[E]   87-31766   CIP   AC

ISBN 0-8234-0689-X
ISBN 0-8234-0798-5 (pbk.)

ISBN-13: 978-0-8234-0689-0 (hardcover)
ISBN-13: 978-0-8234-0798-9 (paperback)

Once upon a time Anansi the Spider was walking, walking, walking through the forest when something caught his eye. It was a strange moss-covered rock.

"How interesting!" Anansi said. "Isn't this a strange moss-covered rock!"

KPOM! Everything went black. Down fell Anansi, sense-less.

An hour later Anansi woke up. His head was spinning. He wondered what had happened.

"I was walking along the path when something caught my eye. I stopped and said, 'Isn't this a strange moss-covered rock.' "

KPOM! Down fell Anansi again. But this time, when he woke up an hour later, he knew what was happening.

"Aha!" said Anansi. "This is a magic rock. And whenever anyone comes along and says the magic words, 'Isn't this a strange hmm-hmmmmm hmm,' down he goes. This is a good thing to know," said Anansi. "And I know just how to use it."

So Anansi went walking, walking, walking through the forest until he came to Lion's house. Lion was sitting on his porch. At his feet was a great pile of yams. Anansi loved yams, but he was too lazy to dig them up himself. Anansi said to Lion, "Hello, Lion! It is very hot today. Don't you think so?"

"Yes, Anansi," said Lion. "It is terribly hot."

"I am going for a walk in the cool forest," said Anansi. "Would you like to come?"

"I certainly would," said Lion.

So Lion and Anansi went walking, walking, walking through the forest. After a while Anansi led Lion to a certain place.

"Lion! Do you see what I see?"

"Oh, yes, Anansi!" said Lion. "Isn't this a strange moss-covered rock!"

KPOM! Down fell Lion. Anansi ran back to Lion's house
and made off with Lion's yams.

An hour later Lion woke up. His head was spinning. Anansi was nowhere in sight. And when he got home, he found that every single one of his yams was gone. Lion was very sad.

But Anansi was very happy. He couldn't wait to play his trick again.

Once more Anansi went walking, walking, walking through the forest. This time he stopped at Elephant's house. Elephant was sitting on his porch. At Elephant's feet was a great pile of bananas. Anansi loved bananas, but he was too lazy to pick them himself. So he said to Elephant, ''Hello, Elephant! Isn't it hot today!''

''It is!'' Elephant agreed.

''I am going for a walk in the cool forest,'' Anansi said. ''Would you like to come?''

''That sounds nice,'' said Elephant. ''Thank you for inviting me, Anansi.''

So Anansi and Elephant went walking, walking, walking through the forest. After a while Anansi led Elephant to a certain place.

"Elephant! Look! Do you see what I see?"

Elephant looked. "Yes I do, Anansi. Isn't this a strange moss-covered rock!"

KPOM! Down fell Elephant. Anansi ran back to Elephant's house and made off with all the bananas.

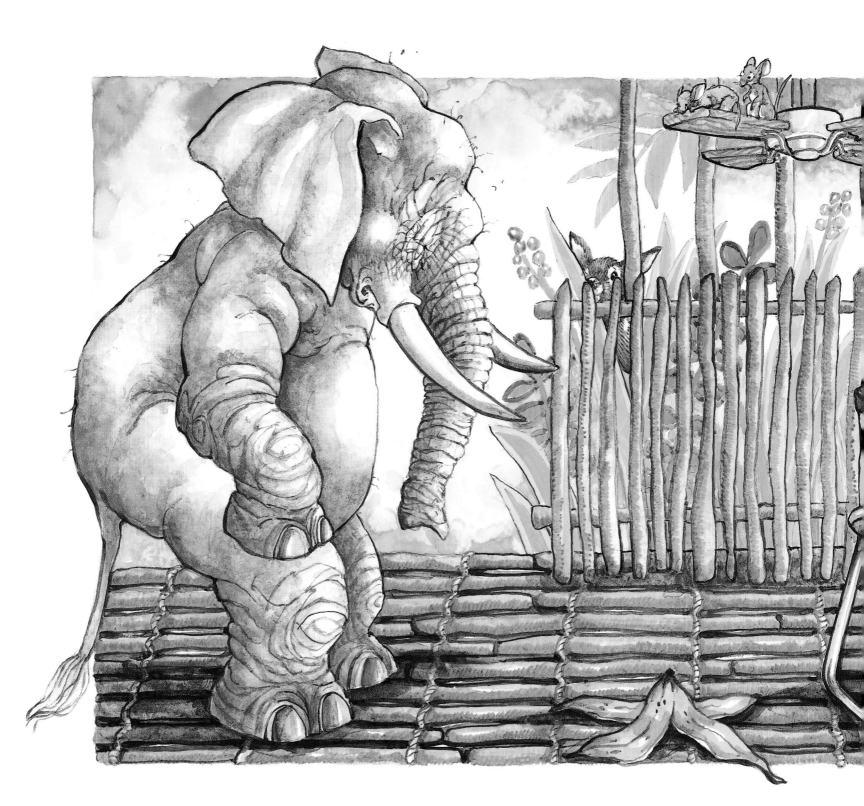

An hour later Elephant woke up. His head was spinning. Anansi was nowhere in sight. And when he got home, he found that every single one of his bananas was gone. Elephant was very sad.

But Anansi was very happy. He couldn't wait to play his
trick again. He played it on Rhinoceros

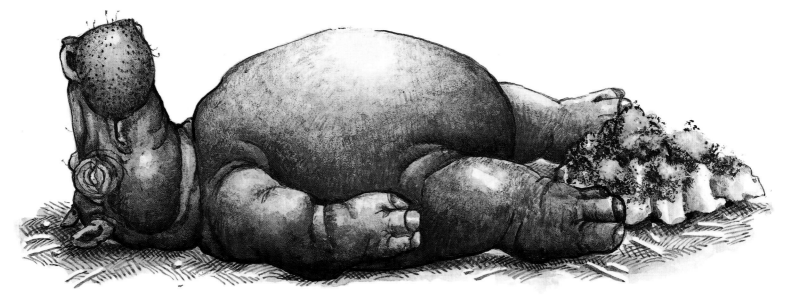

and Hippopotamus.

He played it on Giraffe

and Zebra. He played it on every single animal in the forest.

But all this time, watching from behind the leaves, was Little Bush Deer. Little Bush Deer is small and shy, and very hard to see. She watched Anansi play his wicked trick again and again on all the other animals. Little Bush Deer decided it was time for Anansi to learn a lesson.

So Little Bush Deer went deep into the forest to where the coconut trees grow. She climbed a coconut tree and threw down a great many coconuts. She carried the coconuts home in a basket and set them on her porch. Then she sat down beside them to wait.

In a little while along came Anansi. Anansi's eyes lit up when he saw Little Bush Deer's coconuts. Anansi loved coconuts. He loved to eat the tender white coconut meat and drink the sweet coconut milk inside. But he was much too lazy to gather coconuts himself.

Instead he said, "Hello, Little Bush Deer! It is so hot today!"

Little Bush Deer smiled. "It is very hot, Anansi."

"I am going for a walk in the cool forest. Would you like to come?"

"Yes, I would," said Little Bush Deer.

So Anansi and Little Bush Deer went walking, walking, walking in the cool forest. After a while Anansi led Little Bush Deer to a certain place.

"Little Bush Deer! Look over there! Do you see what I see?"

Little Bush Deer knew all about Anansi's trick. She looked. "No, Anansi. I don't see anything."

"You must see it. Look very carefully."

Little Bush Deer looked. "No. I still don't see anything," she said.

Anansi began to get angry. "You must see it. Look over here. Look right where I'm pointing. Do you see it now?"

"No, Anansi," said Little Bush Deer.

Anansi stamped his legs. "You see it. You just don't want to say it."

"Say what?" said Little Bush Deer.

"You know."

"Is that what I'm supposed to say?"

"Yes," said Anansi.

"All right. Then I will say it to make you happy. 'You know,'" said Little Bush Deer. "There! I said it. Are you satisfied?"

"No!" Anansi shouted. "You're not supposed to say 'You know!'"

"What am I supposed to say?"

"You're supposed to say, 'Isn't this a strange moss-covered rock!'"

KPOM! Down fell Anansi.

Little Bush Deer ran and got all the other animals. Together
they went to Anansi's house and took back all the good things
he had stolen from them.

An hour later Anansi woke up. His head was spinning. Little Bush Deer was nowhere in sight. And when he got home, he found his house as empty as it was before.

But if you think Anansi learned his lesson, you're mistaken. Because he's still playing tricks to this very day.